Peppa Pig™

Daddy Pig's Old Chair

The school roof has a hole in it. "We are going to have a jumble sale," announces Madame Gazelle.

"The money we raise will pay for a new roof."
Everybody has to bring something to sell.

Later, Peppa is in her bedroom choosing a toy to give
to the jumble sale. "Mr Dinosaur!" she decides.

Everybody gasps and George bursts into tears.
"You can't give away Mr Dinosaur," says Mummy Pig.

"Why don't you give your old jack-in-the-box?" suggests Daddy Pig.

"Oh, ok," agrees Peppa.

"Now it's your turn Daddy.

What are you going to give?"

Daddy Pig is not sure.

"What about your old squeaky chair?" suggests Peppa helpfully.

"But it's very old and valuable," says Daddy Pig.
"Hee hee," says Mummy Pig. "You found it
on a rubbish tip!"

When Madame Gazelle arrives in her truck, Mummy Pig, Peppa and George give her everything to take to the jumble sale.

Naughty Mummy Pig gives her Daddy's
squeaky chair too.
"Daddy Pig will never notice,"
she whispers to Peppa.

It is the day of the jumble sale.
There are lots of things to buy.

Mummy Pig wants to buy some fruit and vegetables.
Daddy Pig wants to buy a chocolate cake.

"Peppa," says Miss Rabbit.
"How about buying this chair?
It's a bit of rubbish but you can chop
it up and use it for firewood."

"But Daddy says it's very old and worth lots of money!" says Peppa.

All Peppa's friends have given something to the jumble sale. Suzy has given her nurse's outfit.

Pedro has given his balloon and
Candy has given her skipping rope.

"I will miss my jack-in-the-box," sighs Peppa.
"I will miss playing at nurses," says Suzy sadly.

Peppa's friends all think they will miss their toys,
so they buy them back again.

"Look what I've bought!" snorts Daddy Pig.
"It's an antique chair to match my old one!"

"Oh Daddy Pig!" laughs Mummy Pig.
"It matches your old one because it
IS your old one!" snorts Peppa.

"But Miss Rabbit has just charged me lots
of money for it!" says poor Daddy Pig.
"Fantastic news!" says Madame Gazelle.

"We have just raised all the money
we need for a new school roof!"
"Hooray!" everybody cheers.